Greymalkin
and the baby dragon
The Queen's Cat

Hi Macy,

Oh no! The baby dragon is lost & scared! Is Greymalkin brave enough to help the baby dragon find his way home?

Have fun reading this adventure!

Gail Truax
&
Greymalkin

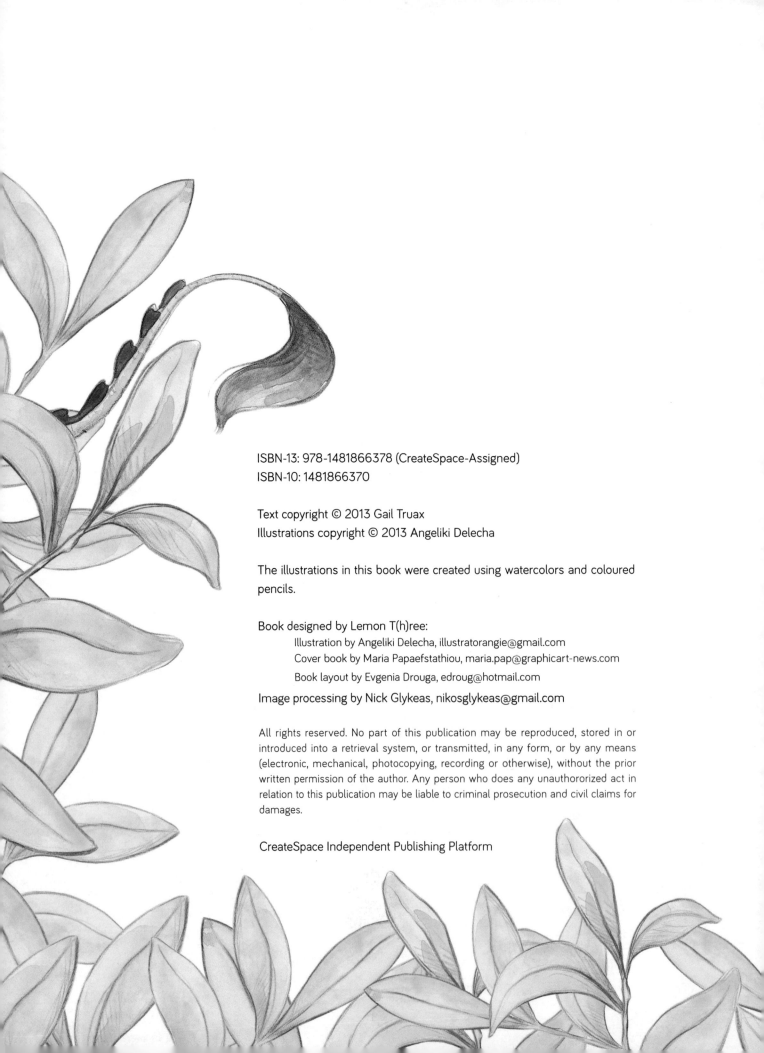

ISBN-13: 978-1481866378 (CreateSpace-Assigned)
ISBN-10: 1481866370

The illustrations in this book were created using watercolors and coloured pencils.

Book designed by Lemon T(h)ree:
    Illustration by Angeliki Delecha, illustratorangie@gmail.com
    Cover book by Maria Papaefstathiou, maria.pap@graphicart-news.com
    Book layout by Evgenia Drouga, edroug@hotmail.com
Image processing by Nick Glykeas, nikosglykeas@gmail.com

CreateSpace Independent Publishing Platform

Greymalkin

The Queen's Cat

and the baby dragon

by Gail Truax

Illustrated by
Angeliki Delecha

Greymalkin decided to take a walk.

The Queen was busy in her study, so he would have to go by himself. With the bright sunshine calling him, he began to stroll through the garden, taking time to carefully inspect the caterpillar crawling slowly up a long green stemmed flower and lifting his face to feel the soft breeze.

Carefully he crossed the small brook, jumping from rock to rock so as to not get his paws wet.

Then he climbed the small hill, crossed the footbridge, and entered the forest.

Greymalkin liked the forest with its trees, quiet places to think, flowers that hid beneath large green leaves, and birds and butterflies to watch fly above and...

wait...
what was that noise?

Greymalkin heard a snuffling, crying sound.

Greymalkin paused and crept quietly forward to discover where the crying was coming from.

To his surprise, it was a baby dragon. Immediately, he backed up and turned to retreat. Going through his mind was that baby dragons were usually followed closely by mommy dragons. Both were to be feared.

The mommy because she was determined not to let anything hurt her baby and the baby because it had not learned to control its mighty powers. But as he was leaving, Greymalkin could feel and hear the little dragon gasping and crying from fear. He could not just leave the baby alone. However, helping a baby dragon could result in serious injuries, so he needed A PLAN.

The **most dangerous** thing about baby dragons was their lack of control. When the baby dragon heard him speak, its first response would probably be a burst of flame. Thinking about this, Greymalkin decided that he would speak and immediately move himself to another area out of range of the flames the baby would emit. Picking his way carefully through the bushes and vines, Greymalkin found a spot close to a tree with high branches. He then leaned slowly forward and said in a soft but clear voice,

"Baby Dragon, what is the matter?"

Then Greymalkin launched himself into the tree and quickly climbed up to a high branch where he could still see the baby dragon.

S tartled, the baby dragon turned toward the voice, belched, and set a small bush afire. Tears streamed down the baby's cheeks as he said in a wavering voice,

"Who is there? Where are you?"

Greymalkin leaned forward and said,

"I am Greymalkin, the Queen's Cat, and I will help you. But, I am afraid you will set me on fire as you did the bush." Then he immediately leapt from the branch he was on to another branch in a nearby tree.

The baby dragon looked up in the tree to find the voice, belched, and set the limb on fire where Greymalkin had been sitting. Seeing nothing, he asked in a tremulous voice, "Where are you? I have heard of Greymalkin. He is a cat of honor and can be trusted. But, when I am afraid I have trouble controlling my fire breath."

Greymalkin asked quietly,

"Where is your mother, baby dragon?"

The baby dragon began to hiccup and said,

"My mommy got losted.
She fell asleep,
and I saw a butterfly
that I wanted to fly with,
but then
the butterfly got losted
and when I tried to
find my mommy,
she was losted too."

Even though
the little dragon
valiantly tried to
hold back his fire
breath, a small
flame leapt out,
and a rock a few
feet from him
explo̵ded
from the heat.

As Greymalkin watched the little dragon trying to keep his fear in check, he said to himself, "Look how brave this little dragon is trying to be. He will be a valiant dragon someday. But today, he's just a lost child." Out loud, he said,

"Baby Dragon, what is your name?"

"Thunder is what my mommy calls me",
the baby dragon replied.

"And what is your mommy's name, little one?"
Greymalkin asked gently.

Thunder replied,
"My mommy's name is Mommy."

Smiling, Greymalkin asked,
"What would I call her, little one?"

Thinking hard, Thunder replied,
"Magenta. You would call my mommy Magenta."

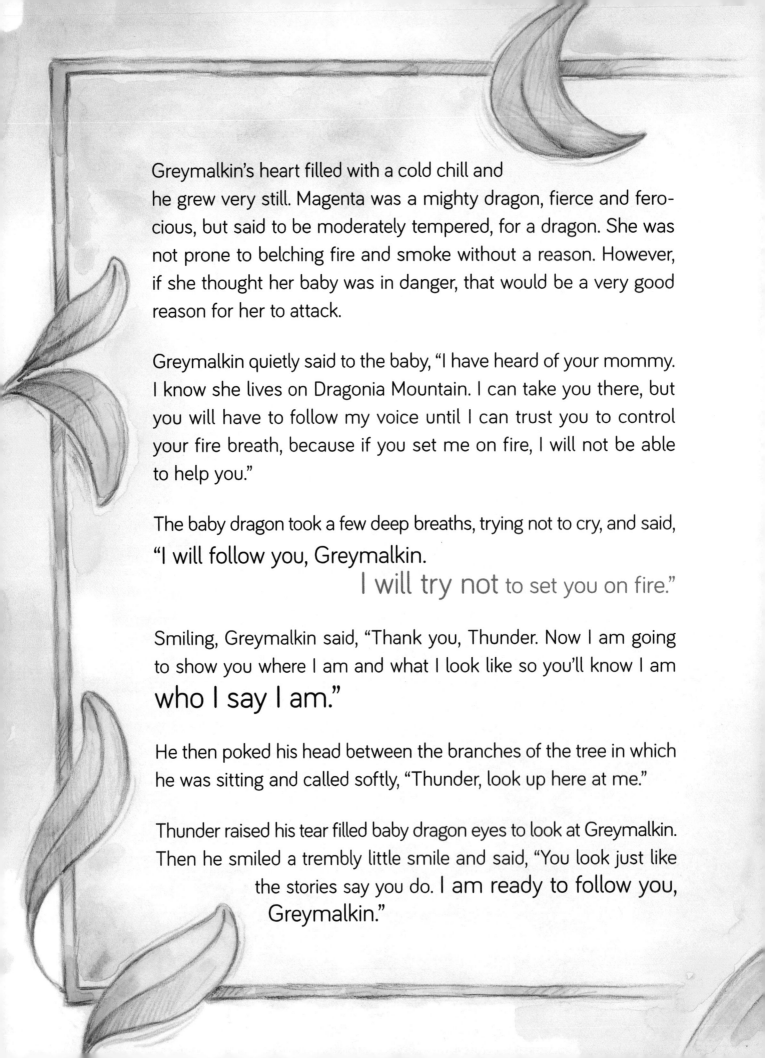

Greymalkin's heart filled with a cold chill and he grew very still. Magenta was a mighty dragon, fierce and ferocious, but said to be moderately tempered, for a dragon. She was not prone to belching fire and smoke without a reason. However, if she thought her baby was in danger, that would be a very good reason for her to attack.

Greymalkin quietly said to the baby, "I have heard of your mommy. I know she lives on Dragonia Mountain. I can take you there, but you will have to follow my voice until I can trust you to control your fire breath, because if you set me on fire, I will not be able to help you."

The baby dragon took a few deep breaths, trying not to cry, and said, "I will follow you, Greymalkin. I will try not to set you on fire."

Smiling, Greymalkin said, "Thank you, Thunder. Now I am going to show you where I am and what I look like so you'll know I am who I say I am."

He then poked his head between the branches of the tree in which he was sitting and called softly, "Thunder, look up here at me."

Thunder raised his tear filled baby dragon eyes to look at Greymalkin. Then he smiled a trembly little smile and said, "You look just like the stories say you do. I am ready to follow you, Greymalkin."

Greymalkin leapt from tree limb to tree limb, calling to Thunder so he could follow his voice. Greymalkin felt very badly for the little dragon, who was still very scared and crying. He remembered hearing stories about a **"Fairy Dragon"** who was supposed to bring good things to little dragons. Thinking that it might help Thunder to calm down if he heard a familiar story Greymalkin asked, "Thunder, I know a story about the Fairy Dragon. Would you like me to tell it to you?"

Thunder said, "My mommy tells me stories about the Fairy Dragon. I like them."

So Greymalkin began to tell a story about the Fairy Dragon. Sometimes he would leave out an important part of the story, so Thunder would correct him asking, "But didn't the Fairy Dragon do this?" or "Didn't the Fairy Dragon say that?" After a while, the little dragon began to calm down and he was no longer crying or as scared as he was before. Greymalkin then asked, "Thunder, do you think you would like for me to walk with you now?"

Thunder replied, "Yes, I would like to walk with you, Greymalkin."

Together the two of them made their way toward Dragonia Mountain. Greymalkin told more Fairy Dragon stories.

Thunder even told Greymalkin a Fairy Dragon story
he had not heard.

The two came to the edge of a high cliff. Greymalkin looked over the edge and asked in wonderment, "Thunder, how did you get up here?"

"I flew," said Thunder.

Greymalkin said, "Well, I cannot fly, so we'll need to look for a path down to the valley."

Thunder said, "OK. Will that take very long?"

Greymalkin replied, "Yes, it probably will because we will have to find a path through the trees."

"Why don't we fly?"
asked Thunder.

"I can't fly,"
replied Greymalkin.

Thunder's bottom lip began to quiver and he said, "But I don't want to walk if it's going to take a long time. I want to go home to my mommy. I want to fly."

Greymalkin looked at Thunder and, not knowing what else to say, repeated, "I can't fly."

Thunder's bottom lip stuck out in a very stubborn fashion as he emphatically declared, "Then you can sit on my back and I'll fly us down to the valley."

Greymalkin's heart fell. His paws became clammy. His throat became dry. In a panic he thought, "This baby dragon wants me to sit on his back while he flies us from the top of this cliff down to and across the valley?" Brave Greymalkin's knees were shaking with fear.

"I don't know how to ride on your back, Thunder. I don't even know how I would get up onto your back," Greymalkin protested.

Thunder looked Greymalkin bravely in the eye and said, "My mommy takes me flying with her sometimes. She lets me climb up her wing and then I sit on her back and we go flying. I bet I could do that with you."

Greymalkin looked at the brave little dragon, took a deep breath, gulped and said, "OK...we'll try it."

Thunder lowered his wing allowing Greymalkin to gingerly place his front paw on his delicate wing. Thunder's wing shook but remained in place. Greymalkin then placed his second paw on the dragon's wing. As Thunder's wing continued to shake, Greymalkin gingerly placed his third and fourth paw on the shaking wing. Thunder's wing began to shake so hard that Greymalkin went flying off into the air, tumbling head over heels and finally falling to the ground, on all four feet, several feet away.

"Thunder, you **shook me off** your wing,"
Greymalkin said.

"It tickles,"
Thunder replied.
"I can't help it. It tickles me when you put your paws on my wings."

Thunder looked at Greymalkin, standing in the dirt a few feet away, and said, "I'll try really hard not to laugh this time Greymalkin."

"OK," Greymalkin agreed, "I'll try again."

So once again Thunder lowered his wing and once again Greymalkin began to climb the baby dragon's wing. He was careful not to extend his claws because the baby dragon's wings were very sensitive, like fine silk or delicate paper. Thunder was having a hard time not laughing, and Greymalkin felt like he was on a swinging bridge. This time, though, he made it onto the baby dragon's back.

As soon as he stepped from the baby dragon's wing onto his back, the shaking stopped.

After a couple of moments, Thunder cried out, "Greymalkin, did you fall off again?"

Greymalkin said, "No, Thunder, I am on your back."

Incredulously, Thunder said, "I cannot feel you at all."

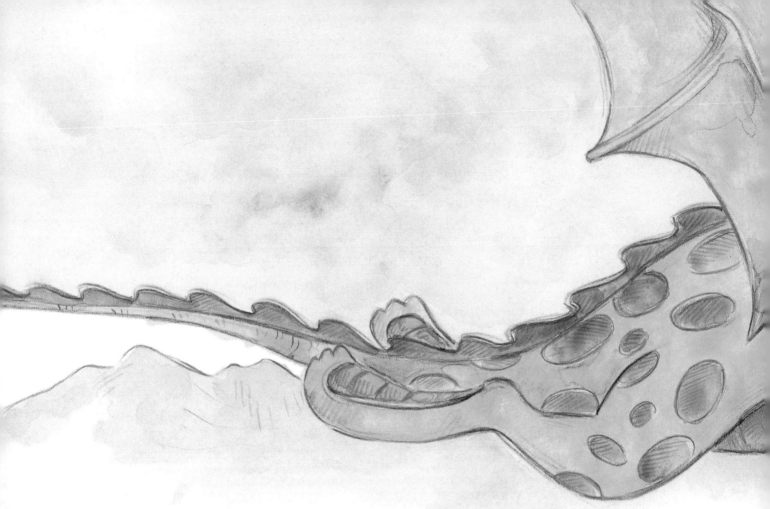

Greymalkin realized that while the baby dragon's wings
were still delicate, the skin on his back was so tough he could not feel
him at all. Then he had an idea. He said to Thunder, "I am going to try
something, and if it hurts even a little bit, you have to tell me so I can
stop."

"What are you going to do?"
asked Thunder.

"I am going to put my claws out to see if I can hold onto your back with
my claws. But if it hurts, you must tell me so I can stop."

"OK", said Thunder.

Greymalkin then extended his claws on his front paws and took a good
hold of Thunder's back. Thunder did not even budge –his skin was so
thick that he could not feel Greymalkin's claws at all. Greymalkin then
extended his back claws and held on tightly to Thunder's back there also.
Greymalkin felt much safer and more secure on Thunder's back now

that he could hang on with his claws. He told Thunder, "I'm ready when you are." Thunder said, "Let's go fly, Greymalkin."

Thunder ran straight toward the edge of the cliff and jumped off into the empty air. Greymalkin caught his breath, shut his eyes, and clung tightly to the little dragon's back. Thunder loved flying, and he swooped joyfully through the air. After a few minutes Greymalkin also enjoyed soaring high in the sky and the sensation of the wind in his face. Thunder called back to Greymalkin, "Would you like to turn a somersault?" Greymalkin said quickly, "No". Greymalkin was doing OK with soaring through the air but he was pretty sure he wanted to stay upright.

Greymalkin leaned forward pointing westward and said in Thunder's ear, "Do you see the three mountains? The farthest one on the right is Dragonia Mountain. That is where you and your mommy live."

Thunder gave a shout of joy and began to fly even faster than before. Greymalkin held on tightly and hoped the baby dragon did not make any fast turns.

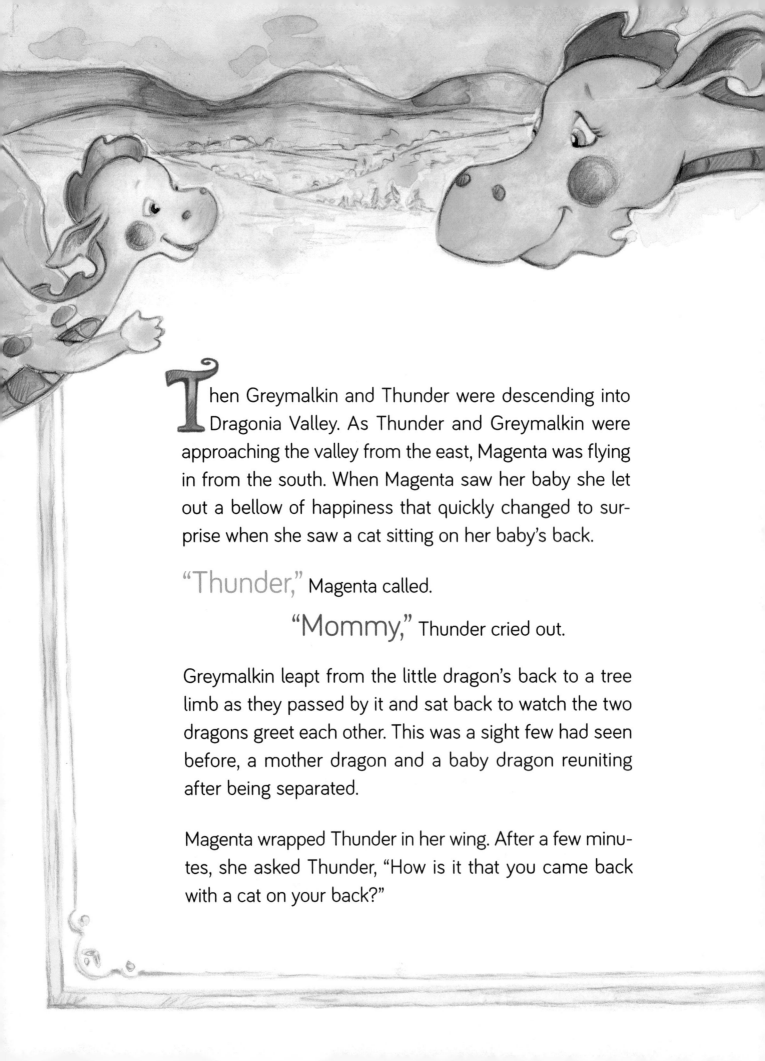

hen Greymalkin and Thunder were descending into Dragonia Valley. As Thunder and Greymalkin were approaching the valley from the east, Magenta was flying in from the south. When Magenta saw her baby she let out a bellow of happiness that quickly changed to surprise when she saw a cat sitting on her baby's back.

"Thunder," Magenta called.

"Mommy," Thunder cried out.

Greymalkin leapt from the little dragon's back to a tree limb as they passed by it and sat back to watch the two dragons greet each other. This was a sight few had seen before, a mother dragon and a baby dragon reuniting after being separated.

Magenta wrapped Thunder in her wing. After a few minutes, she asked Thunder, "How is it that you came back with a cat on your back?"

Thunder looked up at his mommy and said with great pride,
"Mommy, that is Greymalkin, the Queen's Cat.
He found me losted in the forest and brought me back to you.
I let him ride on my back because he cannot fly."

Magenta bent her magnificent head to her child and
tears fell gently on Thunder's head. Dragons are
very particular about letting another being ride
on their back and it is a great honor
to do so. Magenta lifted her head to
Greymalkin and called, "Greymalkin,
the Queen's Cat, I thank you most
profoundly for finding my dragon-ling
and bringing him back to me."

Greymalkin said in his very best courtier's voice,

"O' great Magenta,

Thunder is a great and wonderful dragon-ling.
Someday he will be powerful and mighty and, hopefully,
as wise as his great mother."

Magenta preened, very pleased with Greymalkin's praise of her little son, and asked, "Greymalkin, how is that you will be going home this evening?"

Greymalkin sat up very straight, raised his chin, and said, "I will walk home, Magenta. There are trees to rest in along the way, and water to quench my thirst."

Magenta smiled, recognizing that Greymalkin did not want to be paid for his good deed, and inquired, "But it will be quite late when you arrive at the Queen's castle. Won't she worry about you?"

Greymalkin replied, "Yes, she will. However, I will be there by morning's light and then she will be OK."

Magenta, bowing her head to Greymalkin, said,

"I would be honored, Greymalkin,

the Queen's Cat,
if you would allow me
to fly you back to your Queen."

Greymalkin was very surprised
because he knew
what a great honor it was for Magenta,
one of the greatest dragons to have ever lived,
to offer to let him ride on her back.

They were both surprised when
a wail erupted from Thunder.

"No. You cannot ride on
my mommy's back.

I do not want to be left alone."

Magenta's tongue flashed out as she
licked the baby dragon's cheek and
said quietly, "Thunder, I do believe
my back is broad enough for both
you and Greymalkin to sit on
comfortably for such a
short ride."

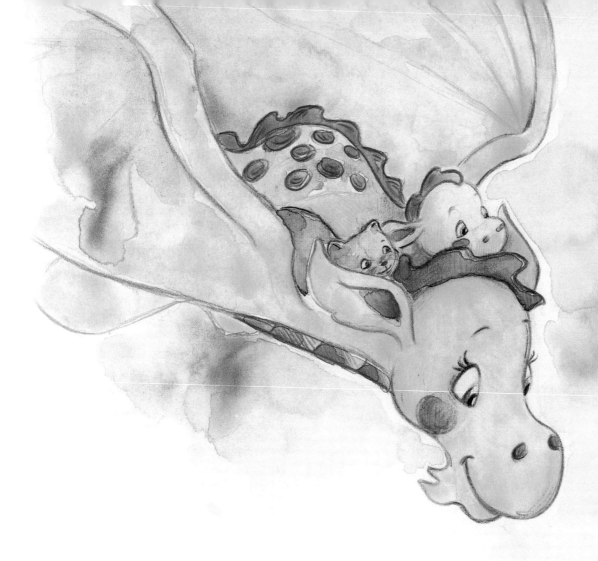

Thunder and Greymalkin both climbed up Magenta's mighty wing and settled themselves onto her broad back. Magenta took off with

a powerful flapping of wings,

soared up high into the sky, over the forest, and in almost no time at all was approaching the Queen's castle.

he Queen's villagers were terrified. A huge dragon was descending upon them. This was almost always disastrous for the village, because usually when a dragon came to visit them, everything for miles around was burnt to the ground. Surprised, the villagers watched as the dragon flew over the village without pausing and headed straight toward the castle before beginning to descend.

The Queen was standing on the castle terrace, wondering where Greymalkin had gone, when a dark shadow passed over her. Looking up she saw a fierce and mighty dragon descending into the garden. The Queen was greatly concerned, because dragons could cause a lot of destruction. But as the dragon flew closer, the Queen leaned forward and could not believe her eyes.

Greymalkin was sitting on this dragon's back and there was a baby dragon beside him.

"Do no harm,"
the Queen called to her men.

Magenta landed gently in the meadow near the castle. She raised her mighty head and looked at the Queen, then dipped her head in reverence to the Queen. Magenta raised her wings, winked at Greymalkin and blew a puff of smoke around his head, then with an impressive flapping of her wings, headed back to Dragonia Mountain.

That puff of smoke
surrounded Greymalkin's head and
looked like a halo.
It was so dense it lasted almost
5
minutes.

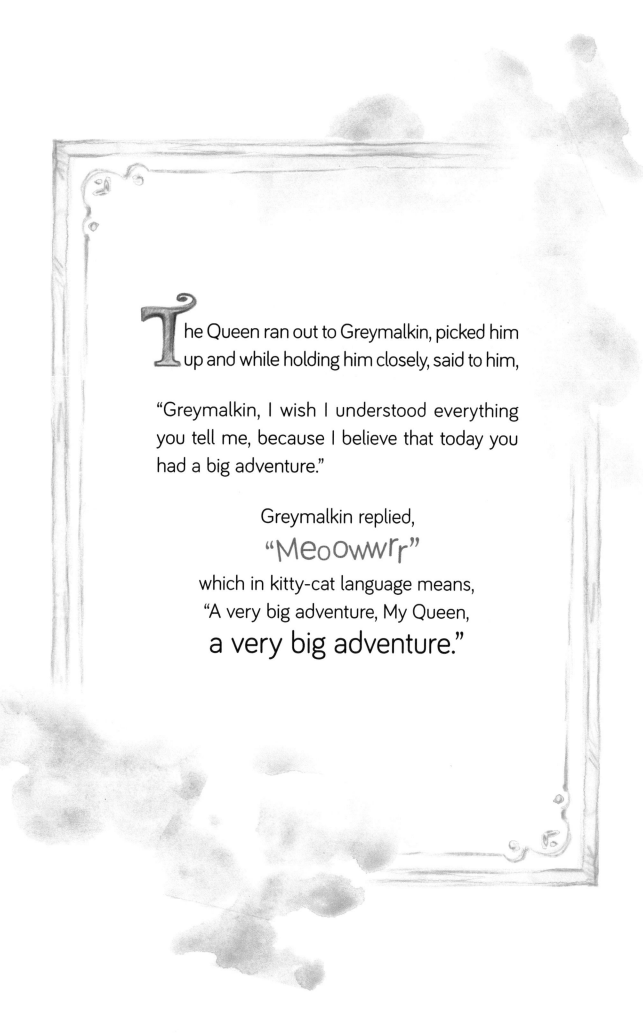

The Queen ran out to Greymalkin, picked him up and while holding him closely, said to him,

"Greymalkin, I wish I understood everything you tell me, because I believe that today you had a big adventure."

Greymalkin replied,
"Meoowwrr"
which in kitty-cat language means,
"A very big adventure, My Queen,
a very big adventure."

This book is dedicated to
my granddaughter Izzy
who helped me reconnect with my inner child
and transformed a story teller into an author.

I hope you enjoy the adventures of Greymalkin
half as much as we have.

Made in the USA
Charleston, SC
18 September 2015